# THE PHOENIX ON THE SWORD

## BY

## ROBERT E. HOWARD

**British Library Cataloguing-in-Publication Data**
A catalogue record for this book is available from the
British Library

# Contents

Robert E. Howard. . . . . . . . . . . . . . . . . . . . . . . . . . . . . . . . . . 1

Chapter I. . . . . . . . . . . . . . . . . . . . . . . . . . . . . . . . . . . . . . . . 3

Chapter II . . . . . . . . . . . . . . . . . . . . . . . . . . . . . . . . . . . . . . 10

Chapter III . . . . . . . . . . . . . . . . . . . . . . . . . . . . . . . . . . . . . 16

Chapter IV . . . . . . . . . . . . . . . . . . . . . . . . . . . . . . . . . . . . . 23

Chapter V . . . . . . . . . . . . . . . . . . . . . . . . . . . . . . . . . . . . . . 27

# Robert E. Howard

Robert Ervin Howard was born in Peaster, Texas in 1906. During his youth, his family moved between a variety of Texan boomtowns, and Howard – a bookish and somewhat introverted child – was steeped in the violent myths and legends of the Old South. Although he loved reading and learning, Howard developed a distinctly Texan, hardboiled outlook on the world. He became a passionate fan of boxing, taking it up at an amateur level, and from the age of nine began to write adventure tales of semi-historical bloodshed. In 1919, when Howard was thirteen, his family moved to the Central Texas hamlet of Cross Plains, where he would stay for the rest of his life.

At fifteen Howard began to read the pulp magazines of the day, and to write more seriously. The December 1922 issue of his high school newspaper featured two of his stories, 'Golden Hope Christmas' and 'West is West'. In 1924 he sold his first piece – a short caveman tale titled 'Spear and Fang' – for $16 to the not-yet-famous *Weird Tales* magazine. He published with the magazine regularly over the next few years. 1929 was a breakout year for Howard, in that the 23-year-old writer began to sell to other magazines, such as *Ghost Stories* and *Argosy*, both of whom had previously sent him hundreds of rejection slips. In 1930, he began a correspondence with weird fiction master H. P. Lovecraft which ran up to his death six years later, and is regarded as one of the great correspondence cycles in all of fantasy literature.

It was partly due to Lovecraft's encouragement that Howard created his most famous character, Conan the Cimmerian. Conan – a barbarian-turned-King during the Hyborian Age, a mythical period of some 12,000 years ago – featured in seventeen *Weird Tales* stories between 1933 and 1936, and is now regarded as having spawned the 'sword and sorcery' genre, making Howard's influence on fantasy literature comparable to that of J. R. R. Tolkien's. The Conan stories have since been adapted many times, most famously in the series of films starring Arnold Schwarzenegger.

Howard was enjoying an all-time high in sales by the beginning of 1936, but he was also deeply upset by the ill health of his mother, who had fallen into a coma. On the morning of June 11, 1936, he asked an attending nurse whether she would ever recover, and the nurse replied negatively. Howard walked to his car, parked outside the family home in Cross Plains, and shot himself. He died eight hours later, aged just thirty.

# CHAPTER I

"Know, oh prince, that between the years when the oceans drank Atlantis and the gleaming cities, and the years of the rise of the Sons of Aryas, there was an Age undreamed of, when shining kingdoms lay spread across the world like blue mantles beneath the stars — Nemedia, Ophir, Brythunia, Hyperborea, Zamora with its dark-haired women and towers of spider-haunted mystery, Zingara with its chivalry, Koth that bordered on the pastoral lands of Shem, Stygia with its shadow-guarded tombs, Hyrkania whose riders wore steel and silk and gold. But the proudest kingdom of the world was Aquilonia, reigning supreme in the dreaming west. Hither came Conan, the Cimmerian, black-haired, sullen-eyed, sword in hand, a thief, a reaver, a slayer, with gigantic melancholies and gigantic mirth, to tread the jeweled thrones of the Earth under his sandalled feet."

— *The Nemedian Chronicles.*

Over shadowy spires and gleaming towers lay the ghostly darkness and silence that runs before dawn. Into a dim alley, one of a veritable labyrinth of mysterious winding ways, four masked figures came hurriedly from a door which a dusky hand furtively opened. They spoke not but went swiftly into the gloom, cloaks wrapped closely about them; as silently as the ghosts of murdered men they disappeared in the darkness. Behind them a sardonic countenance was framed in the partly opened door; a pair of evil eyes glittered malevolently in the gloom.

"Go into the night, creatures of the night," a voice mocked. "Oh, fools, your doom hounds your heels like a blind dog, and you know it not."

The speaker closed the door and bolted it, then turned and went up the corridor, candle in hand. He was a somber giant, whose dusky skin revealed his Stygian blood. He came into an inner chamber, where a tall, lean man in worn velvet lounged like a great lazy cat on a silken couch, sipping wine from a huge golden goblet.

"Well, Ascalante," said the Stygian, setting down the candle, "your dupes have slunk into the streets like rats from their burrows. You work with strange tools."

"Tools?" replied Ascalante. "Why, they consider *me* that. For months now, ever since the Rebel Four summoned me from the southern desert, I have been living in the very heart of my enemies, hiding by day in this obscure house, skulking through dark alleys and darker corridors at night. And I have accomplished what those rebellious nobles could not. Working through them, and through other agents, many of whom have never seen my face, I have honeycombed the empire with sedition and unrest. In short I, working in the shadows, have paved the downfall of the king who sits throned in the sun. By Mitra, I was a statesman before I was an outlaw."

"And these dupes who deem themselves your masters?"

"They will continue to think that I serve them, until our present task is completed. Who are they to match wits with Ascalante? Volmana, the dwarfish count of Karaban; Gromel, the giant commander of the Black Legion; Dion, the fat baron of Attalus; Rinaldo, the hare-brained minstrel. I am the force which has welded together the steel in each, and by the clay in each, I will crush them when the time comes. But that lies in the future; tonight the king dies."

"Days ago I saw the imperial squadrons ride from the city," said the Stygian.

"They rode to the frontier which the heathen Picts assail — thanks to the strong liquor which I've smuggled over the borders to madden them. Dion's great wealth made that possible. And Volmana made it possible to dispose of the rest of the imperial troops which remained in the city. Through his princely kin in Nemedia, it was easy to persuade King Numa to request the presence of Count Trocero of Poitain, seneschal of Aquilonia; and of course, to do him honor, he'll be accompanied by an imperial escort, as well as his own troops, and Prospero, King Conan's right hand man. That leaves only the king's personal bodyguard in the city-beside the Black Legion. Through Gromel I've corrupted a spendthrift officer of that guard, and bribed him to lead his men away from the king's door at midnight.

"Then, with sixteen desperate rogues of mine, we enter the palace by a secret tunnel. After the deed is done, even if the people do not rise to welcome us, Gromel's Black Legion will be sufficient to hold the city and the crown."

"And Dion thinks that crown will be given to him?"

"Yes. The fat fool claims it by reason of a trace of royal blood. Conan makes a bad mistake in letting men live who still boast descent from the old dynasty, from which he tore the crown of Aquilonia.

"Volmana wishes to be reinstated in royal favor as he was under the old regime, so that he may lift his poverty-ridden estates to their former grandeur. Gromel hates Pallantides, commander of the Black Dragons, and desires the command of the whole army, with all the stubbornness of the Bossonian. Alone of us all, Rinaldo has no personal ambition. He sees in Conan a red-handed, rough-footed barbarian who came out of the north to plunder a civilized land. He idealizes the king whom Conan killed to get the crown, remembering only that he occasionally patronized the arts, and forgetting the evils of his reign, and he is making the people forget. Already they openly sing *The Lament for the King* in which

Rinaldo lauds the sainted villain and denounces Conan as 'that black-hearted savage from the abyss.' Conan laughs, but the people snarl."

"Why does he hate Conan?"

"Poets always hate those in power. To them perfection is always just behind the last corner, or beyond the next. They escape the present in dreams of the past and future. Rinaldo is a flaming torch of idealism, rising, as he thinks, to overthrow a tyrant and liberate the people. As for me — well, a few months ago I had lost all ambition but to raid the caravans for the rest of my life; now old dreams stir. Conan will die; Dion will mount the throne. Then he, too, will die. One by one, all who oppose me will die — by fire, or steel, or those deadly wines you know so well how to brew. Ascalante, king of Aquilonia! How like you the sound of it?"

The Stygian shrugged his broad shoulders.

"There was a time," he said with unconcealed bitterness, "when I, too, had my ambitions, beside which yours seem tawdry and childish. To what a state I have fallen! My old-time peers and rivals would stare indeed could they see Thoth-amon of the Ring serving as the slave of an outlander, and an outlaw at that; and aiding in the petty ambitions of barons and kings!"

"You laid your trust in magic and mummery," answered Ascalante carelessly. "I trust my wits and my sword."

"Wits and swords are as straws against the wisdom of the Darkness," growled the Stygian, his dark eyes flickering with menacing lights and shadows. "Had I not lost the Ring, our positions might be reversed."

"Nevertheless," answered the outlaw impatiently, "you wear the stripes of my whip on your back, and are likely to continue to wear them."

"Be not so sure!" the fiendish hatred of the Stygian glittered for an instant redly in his eyes. "Some day, somehow, I will find the Ring again, and when I do, by the serpent-fangs of Set, you shall pay—"

The hot-tempered Aquilonian started up and struck him heavily across the mouth. Thoth reeled back, blood starting from his lips.

"You grow over-bold, dog," growled the outlaw. "Have a care; I am still your master who knows your dark secret. Go upon the housetops and shout that Ascalante is in the city plotting against the king — if you dare."

"I dare not," muttered the Stygian, wiping the blood from his lips.

"No, you do not dare," Ascalante grinned bleakly. "For if I die by your stealth or treachery, a hermit priest in the southern desert will know of it, and will break the seal of a manuscript I left in his hands. And having read, a word will be whispered in Stygia, and a wind will creep up from the south by midnight. And where will you hide your head, Thoth-amon?"

The slave shuddered and his dusky face went ashen.

"Enough!" Ascalante changed his tone peremptorily. "I have work for you. I do not trust Dion. I bade him ride to his country estate and remain there until the work tonight is done. The fat fool could never conceal his nervousness before the king today. Ride after him, and if you do not overtake him on the road, proceed to his estate and remain with him until we send for him. Don't let him out of your sight. He is mazed with fear, and might bolt — might even rush to Conan in a panic, and reveal the whole plot, hoping thus to save his own hide. Go!"

The slave bowed, hiding the hate in his eyes, and did as he was bidden. Ascalante turned again to his wine. Over the jeweled spires was rising a dawn crimson as blood.

# CHAPTER II

The room was large and ornate, with rich tapestries on the polished-panelled walls, deep rugs on the ivory floor, and with the lofty ceiling adorned with intricate carvings and silver scrollwork. Behind an ivory, gold-inlaid writing-table sat a man whose broad shoulders and sun-browned skin seemed out of place among those luxuriant surroundings. He seemed more a part of the sun and winds and high places of the outlands. His slightest movement spoke of steel-spring muscles knit to a keen brain with the co-ordination of a born fighting-man. There was nothing deliberate or measured about his actions. Either he was perfectly at rest—still as a bronze statue—or else he was in motion, not with the jerky quickness of over-tense nerves, but with a cat-like speed that blurred the sight which tried to follow him.

His garments were of rich fabric, but simply made. He wore no ring or ornaments, and his square-cut black mane was confined merely by a cloth-of-silver band about his head.

Now he laid down the golden stylus with which he had been laboriously scrawling on waxed papyrus, rested his chin on his fist, and fixed his smoldering blue eyes enviously on the man who stood before him. This person was occupied in his own affairs at the moment, for he was taking up the laces of his gold-chased armor, and abstractedly whistling—a rather unconventional performance, considering that he was in the presence of a king.

"Prospero," said the man at the table, "these matters of statecraft weary me as all the fighting I have done never did."

"All part of the game, Conan," answered the dark-eyed Poitainian. "You are king—you must play the part."

"I wish I might ride with you to Nemedia," said Conan enviously. "It seems ages since I had a horse between my knees—but Publius says that affairs in the city require my presence. Curse him!

"When I overthrew the old dynasty," he continued, speaking with the easy familiarity which existed only between the Poitainian and himself, "it was easy enough, though it seemed bitter hard at the time. Looking back now over the wild path I followed, all those days of toil, intrigue, slaughter and tribulation seem like a dream.

"I did not dream far enough, Prospero. When King Numedides lay dead at my feet and I tore the crown from his gory head and set it on my own, I had reached the ultimate border of my dreams. I had prepared myself to take the crown, not to hold it. In the old free days all I wanted was a sharp sword and a straight path to my enemies. Now no paths are straight and my sword is useless.

"When I overthrew Numedides, then I was the Liberator—now they spit at my shadow. They have put a statue of that swine in the temple of Mitra, and people go and wail before it, hailing it as the holy effigy of a saintly monarch who was done to death by a red-handed barbarian. When I led her armies to victory as a mercenary, Aquilonia overlooked the fact that I was a foreigner, but now she can not forgive me.

"Now in Mitra's temple there come to burn incense to Numedides' memory, men whom his hangmen maimed and blinded, men whose sons died in his dungeons, whose wives and daughters were dragged into his seraglio. The fickle fools!"

"Rinaldo is largely responsible," answered Prospero, drawing up his sword-belt another notch. "He sings songs that make men mad. Hang him in his jester's garb to the highest tower in the city. Let him make rimes for the vultures."

Conan shook his lion head. "No, Prospero, he's beyond my reach. A great poet is greater than any king. His songs are mightier than my scepter; for he has near ripped the heart from my breast when he chose to sing for me. I shall die and be forgotten, but Rinaldo's songs will live for ever.

"No, Prospero," the king continued, a somber look of doubt shadowing his eyes, "there is something hidden, some undercurrent of which we are not aware. I sense it as in my youth I sensed the tiger hidden in the tall grass. There is a nameless unrest throughout the kingdom. I am like a hunter who crouches by his small fire amid the forest, and hears stealthy feet padding in the darkness, and almost sees the glimmer of burning eyes. If I could but come to grips with something tangible, that I could cleave with my sword! I tell you, it's not by chance that the Picts have of late so fiercely assailed the frontiers, so that the Bossonians have called for aid to beat them back. I should have ridden with the troops."

"Publius feared a plot to trap and slay you beyond the frontier," replied Prospero, smoothing his silken surcoat over his shining mail, and admiring his tall lithe figure in a silver mirror. "That's why he urged you to remain in the city. These doubts are born of your barbarian instincts. Let the people snarl! The mercenaries are ours, and the Black Dragons, and every rogue in Poitain swears by you. Your only danger is assassination, and that's impossible, with men of the imperial troops guarding you day and night. What are you working at there?"

"A map," Conan answered with pride. "The maps of the court show well the countries of south, east and west, but in the north they are vague and faulty. I am adding the northern lands myself. Here is Cimmeria, where I was born. And—"

"Asgard and Vanaheim," Prospero scanned the map. "By Mitra, I had almost believed those countries to have been fabulous."

Conan grinned savagely, involuntarily touching the scars on his dark face. "You had known otherwise, had you spent your youth on the northern frontiers of Cimmeria! Asgard lies to the north, and Vanaheim to the northwest of Cimmeria, and there is continual war along the borders."

"What manner of men are these northern folk?" asked Prospero.

"Tall and fair and blue-eyed. Their god is Ymir, the frost-giant, and each tribe has its own king. They are wayward and fierce. They fight all day and drink ale and roar their wild songs all night."

"Then I think you are like them," laughed Prospero. "You laugh greatly, drink deep and bellow good songs; though I never saw another Cimmerian who drank aught but water, or who ever laughed, or ever sang save to chant dismal dirges."

"Perhaps it's the land they live in," answered the king. "A gloomier land never was—all of hills, darkly wooded, under skies nearly always gray, with winds moaning drearily down the valleys."

"Little wonder men grow moody there," quoth Prospero with a shrug of his shoulders, thinking of the smiling sun-washed plains and blue lazy rivers of Poitain, Aquilonia's southernmost province.

"They have no hope here or hereafter," answered Conan. "Their gods are Crom and his dark race, who rule over a sunless place of everlasting mist, which is the world of the dead. Mitra! The ways of the Æsir were more to my liking."

"Well," grinned Prospero, "the dark hills of Cimmeria are far behind you. And now I go. I'll quaff a goblet of white Nemedian wine for you at Numa's court."

"Good," grunted the king, "but kiss Numa's dancing-girls for yourself only, lest you involve the states!"

His gusty laughter followed Prospero out of the chamber.

# CHAPTER III

The sun was setting, etching the green and hazy blue of the forest in brief gold. The waning beams glinted on the thick golden chain which Dion of Attalus twisted continually in his pudgy hand as he sat in the flaming riot of blossoms and flower -trees which was his garden. He shifted his fat body on his marble seat and glanced furtively about, as if in quest of a lurking enemy. He sat within a circular grove of slender trees, whose interlapping branches cast a thick shade over him. Near at hand a fountain tinkled silverly, and other unseen fountains in various parts of the great garden whispered an everlasting symphony.

Dion was alone except for the great dusky figure which lounged on a marble bench close at hand, watching the baron with deep somber eyes. Dion gave little thought to Thoth-amon. He vaguely knew that he was a slave in whom Ascalante reposed much trust, but like so many rich men, Dion paid scant heed to men below his own station in life.

"You need not be so nervous," said Thoth. "The plot can not fail."

"Ascalante can make mistakes as well as another," snapped Dion, sweating at the mere thought of failure.

"Not he," grinned the Stygian savagely, "else I had not been his slave, but his master."

"What talk is this?" peevishly returned Dion, with only half a mind on the conversation.

Thoth-amon's eyes narrowed. For all his iron-self-control, he was near bursting with long pent-up shame, hate and rage, ready to take any sort of a desperate chance. What he did not reckon on was the fact that Dion saw him, not as a human being with a brain and a wit, but simply a slave, and as such, a creature beneath notice.

"Listen to me," said Thoth. "You will be king. But you little know the mind of Ascalante. You can not trust him, once Conan is slain. I can help you. If you will protect me when you come to power, I will aid you.

"Listen, my lord. I was a great sorcerer in the south. Men spoke of Thoth amon as they spoke of Rammon. King Ctesphon of Stygia gave me great honor, casting down the magicians from the high places to exalt me above them. They hated me, but they feared me, for I controlled beings from outside which came at my call and did my bidding. By Set, mine enemy knew not the hour when he might awake at midnight to feel the taloned fingers of a nameless horror at his throat! I did dark and terrible magic with the Serpent Ring of Set, which I found in a nighted tomb a league beneath the earth, forgotten before the first man crawled out of the slimy sea.

"But a thief stole the Ring and my power was broken. The magicians rose up to slay me, and I fled. Disguised as a camel-driver, I was travelling in a caravan in the land of Koth, when Ascalante's reavers fell upon us. All in the caravan were slain except myself; I saved my life by revealing my identity to Ascalante and swearing to serve him. Bitter has been that bondage!

"To hold me fast, he wrote of me in a manuscript, and sealed it and gave it into the hands of a hermit who dwells on the southern borders of Koth. I dare not strike a dagger into him while he sleeps, or betray him to his enemies, for then the hermit would open the manuscript and read—thus Ascalante instructed him. And he would speak a word in Stygia—"

Again Thoth shuddered and an ashen hue tinged his dusky skin.

"Men knew me not in Aquilonia," he said. "But should my enemies in Stygia learn my whereabouts, not the width of half a world between us would suffice to save me from such a doom as would blast the soul of a bronze statue. Only a king with castles and hosts of swordsmen could protect me. So I have told you my secret, and urge that you make a pact with me. I can aid you with my wisdom, and you can protect me. And some day I will find the Ring—"

"Ring? Ring?" Thoth had underestimated the man's utter egoism. Dion had not even been listening to the slave's words, so completely engrossed was he in his own thoughts, but the final word stirred a ripple in his self-centeredness.

"Ring?" he repeated. "That makes me remember—my ring of good fortune. I had it from a Shemitish thief who swore he stole it from a wizard far to the south, and that it would bring me luck. I paid him enough, Mitra knows. By the gods, I need all the luck I can have, what with Volmana and Ascalante dragging me into their bloody plots—I'll see to the ring."

Thoth sprang up, blood mounting darkly to his face, while his eyes flamed with the stunned fury of a man who suddenly realizes the full depths of a fool's swinish stupidity. Dion never heeded him. Lifting a secret lid in the marble seat, he fumbled for a moment among a heap of gewgaws of various kinds—barbaric charms, bits of bones, pieces of tawdry jewelry—luck-pieces and conjures which the man's superstitious nature had prompted him to collect.

"Ah, here it is!" He triumphantly lifted a ring of curious make. It was of a metal like copper, and was made in the form of a scaled serpent, coiled in three loops, with its tail in its mouth. Its eyes were yellow gems which glittered balefully. Thoth-amon cried out as if he had been struck, and Dion wheeled and gaped, his face suddenly bloodless. The slave's eyes were blazing, his mouth wide, his huge dusky hands outstretched like talons.

"The Ring! By Set! The Ring!" he shrieked. "My Ring—stolen from me—" Steel glittered in the Stygian's hand and with a heave of his great dusky shoulders he drove the dagger into the baron's fat body. Dion's high thin squeal broke in a strangled gurgle and his whole flabby frame collapsed like melted butter. A fool to the end, he died in mad terror, not knowing why. Flinging aside the crumpled corpse, already forgetful of it, Thoth grasped the ring in both hands, his dark eyes blazing with a fearful avidness.

"My Ring!" he whispered in terrible exultation. "My power!"

How long he crouched over the baleful thing, motionless as a statue, drinking the evil aura of it into his dark soul, not even the Stygian knew. When he shook himself from his revery and drew back his mind from the nighted abysses where it had been questing, the moon was rising, casting long shadows across the smooth marble back of the garden-seat, at the foot of which sprawled the darker shadow which had been the lord of Attalus.

"No more, Ascalante, no more!" whispered the Stygian, and his eyes burned red as a vampire's in the gloom. Stooping, he cupped a handful of congealing blood from the sluggish pool in which his victim sprawled, and rubbed it in the copper serpent's eyes until the yellow sparks were covered by a crimson mask.

"Blind your eyes, mystic serpent," he chanted in a blood-freezing whisper. "Blind your eyes to the moonlight and open them on darker gulfs! What do you see, oh serpent of Set? Whom do you call from the gulfs of the Night?

Whose shadow falls on the waning Light? Call him to me, oh serpent of Set!"

Stroking the scales with a peculiar circular motion of his fingers, a motion which always carried the fingers back to their starting place, his voice sank still lower as he whispered dark names and grisly incantations forgotten the world over save in the grim hinterlands of dark Stygia, where monstrous shapes move in the dusk of the tombs.

There was a movement in the air about him, such a swirl as is made in water when some creature rises to the surface. A nameless, freezing wind blew on him briefly, as if from an opened Door. Thoth felt a presence at his back, but he did not look about. He kept his eyes fixed on the moonlit space of marble, on which a tenuous shadow hovered. As he continued his whispered incantations, this shadow grew in size and clarity, until it stood out distinct and horrific. Its outline was not unlike that of a gigantic baboon, but no such baboon ever walked the earth, not even in Stygia. Still Thoth did not look, but drawing from his girdle a sandal of his master—always carried in the dim hope that he might be able to put it to such use—he cast it behind him.

"Know it well, slave of the Ring!" he exclaimed. "Find him who wore it and destroy him! Look into his eyes and blast his soul, before you tear out his throat! Kill him! Aye," in a blind burst of passion, "and all with him!"

Etched on the moonlit wall Thoth saw the horror lower its misshapen head and take the scent like some hideous hound. Then the grisly head was thrown back and the thing wheeled and was gone like a wind through the trees. The Stygian flung up his arms in maddened exultation, and his teeth and eyes gleamed in the moonlight.

A soldier on guard without the walls yelled in startled horror as a great loping black shadow with flaming eyes cleared the wall and swept by him with a swirling rush of wind. But it was gone so swiftly that the bewildered warrior was left wondering whether it had been a dream or a hallucination.

# CHAPTER IV

Alone in the great sleeping-chamber with its high golden dome King Conan slumbered and dreamed. Through swirling gray mists he heard a curious call, faint and far, and though he did not understand it, it seemed not within his power to ignore it. Sword in hand he went through the gray mist, as a man might walk through clouds, and the voice grew more distinct as he proceeded until he understood the word it spoke—it was his own name that was being called across the gulfs of Space or Time.

Now the mists grew lighter and he saw that he was in a great dark corridor that seemed to be cut in solid black stone. It was unlighted, but by some magic he could see plainly. The floor, ceiling and walls were highly polished and gleamed dull, and they were carved with the figures of ancient heroes and half-forgotten gods. He shuddered to see the vast shadowy outlines of the Nameless Old Ones, and he knew somehow that mortal feet had not traversed the corridor for centuries.

He came upon a wide stair carved in the solid rock, and the sides of the shaft were adorned with esoteric symbols so ancient and horrific that King Conan's skin crawled. The steps were carven each with the abhorrent figure of the Old Serpent, Set, so that at each step he planted his heel on the head of the Snake, as it was intended from old times. But he was none the less at ease for all that.

But the voice called him on, and at last, in darkness that would have been impenetrable to his material eyes, he came into a strange crypt, and saw a vague white-bearded figure sitting on a tomb. Conan's hair rose up and he grasped his sword, but the figure spoke in sepulchral tones.

"Oh man, do you know me?"

"Not I, by Crom!" swore the king.

"Man," said the ancient, "I am Epemitreus."

"But Epemitreus the Sage has been dead for fifteen hundred years!" stammered Conan.

"Harken!" spoke the other commandingly. "As a pebble cast into a dark lake sends ripples to the further shores, happenings in the Unseen world have broken like waves on my slumber. I have marked you well, Conan of Cimmeria, and the stamp of mighty happenings and great deeds is upon you. But dooms are loose in the land, against which your sword can not aid you."

"You speak in riddles," said Conan uneasily. "Let me see my foe and I'll cleave his skull to the teeth."

"Loose your barbarian fury against your foes of flesh and blood," answered the ancient. "It is not against men I must shield you. There are dark worlds barely guessed by man, wherein formless monsters stalk—fiends which may be drawn from the Outer Voids to take material shape and rend and devour at the bidding of evil magicians. There is a serpent in your house, oh king—an adder in your kingdom, come up from Stygia, with the dark wisdom of the shadows in his murky soul. As a sleeping man dreams of the serpent which crawls near him, I have felt the foul presence of Set's neophyte. He is drunk with terrible power, and the blows he strikes at his enemy may well bring down the kingdom. I have called you to me, to give you a weapon against him and his hell-hound pack."

"But why?" bewilderedly asked Conan. "Men say you sleep in the black heart of Golamira, whence you send forth your ghost on unseen wings to aid Aquilonia in times of need, but I—I am an outlander and a barbarian."

"Peace!" the ghostly tones reverberated through the great shadowy cavern. "Your destiny is one with Aquilonia. Gigantic happenings are forming in the web and the womb of Fate, and a blood-mad sorcerer shall not stand in the path of imperial destiny. Ages ago Set coiled about the world like a python about its prey. All my life, which was as the lives of three common men, I fought him. I drove him into the shadows of the mysterious south, but in dark Stygia men still worship him who to us is the arch-demon. As I fought Set, I fight his worshippers and his votaries and his acolytes. Hold out your sword."

Wondering, Conan did so, and on the great blade, close to the heavy silver guard, the ancient traced with a bony finger a strange symbol that glowed like white fire in the shadows. And on the instant crypt, tomb and ancient vanished, and Conan, bewildered, sprang from his couch in the great golden-domed chamber. And as he stood, bewildered at the strangeness of his dream, he realized that he was gripping his sword in his hand. And his hair prickled at the nape of his neck, for on the broad blade was carven a symbol—the outline of a phœnix. And he remembered that on the tomb in the crypt he had seen what he had thought to be a similar figure, carven of stone. Now he wondered if it had been but a stone figure, and his skin crawled at the strangeness of it all.

Then as he stood, a stealthy sound in the corridor outside brought him to life, and without stopping to investigate, he began to don his armor; again he was the barbarian, suspicious and alert as a gray wolf at bay.

# CHAPTER V

Through the silence which shrouded the corridor of the royal palace stole twenty furtive figures. Their stealthy feet, bare or cased in soft leather, made no sound either on thick carpet or bare marble tile. The torches which stood in niches along the halls gleamed red on dagger, sword and keen-edged ax.

"Easy all!" hissed Ascalante. "Stop that cursed loud breathing, whoever it is! The officer of the night-guard has removed most of the sentries from these halls and made the rest drunk, but we must be careful, just the same. Back! Here come the guard!"

They crowded back behind a cluster of carven pillars, and almost immediately ten giants in black armor swung by at a measured pace. Their faces showed doubt as they glanced at the officer who was leading them away from their post of duty. This officer was rather pale; as the guard passed the hiding-places of the conspirators, he was seen to wipe the sweat from his brow with a shaky hand. He was young, and this betrayal of a king did not come easy to him. He mentally cursed the vain-glorious extravagance which had put him in debt to the money-lenders and made him a pawn of scheming politicians.

The guardsmen clanked by and disappeared up the corridor.

"Good!" grinned Ascalante. "Conan sleeps unguarded. Haste! If they catch us killing him, we're undone—but few men will espouse the cause of a dead king."

"Aye, haste!" cried Rinaldo, his blue eyes matching the gleam of the sword he swung above his head. "My blade is thirsty! I hear the gathering of the vultures! On!"

They hurried down the corridor with reckless speed and stopped before a gilded door which bore the royal dragon symbol of Aquilonia.

"Gromel!" snapped Ascalante. "Break me this door open!"

The giant drew a deep breath and launched his mighty frame against the panels, which groaned and bent at the impact. Again he crouched and plunged. With a snapping of bolts and a rending crash of wood, the door splintered and burst inward.

"In!" roared Ascalante, on fire with the spirit of the deed.

"In!" yelled Rinaldo. "Death to the tyrant!"

They stopped short. Conan faced them, not a naked man roused mazed and unarmed out of deep sleep to be butchered like a sheep, but a barbarian wide-awake and at bay, partly armored, and with his long sword in his hand.

For an instant the tableau held—the four rebel noblemen in the broken door, and the horde of wild hairy faces crowding behind them—all held momentarily frozen by the sight of the blazing-eyed giant standing sword in hand in the middle of the candle-lighted chamber. In that instant Ascalante beheld, on a small table near the royal couch, the silver scepter and the slender gold circlet which was the crown of Aquilonia, and the sight maddened him with desire.

"In, rogues!" yelled the outlaw. "He is one to twenty and he has no helmet!"

True; there had been lack of time to don the heavy plumed casque, or to lace in place the side-plates of the cuirass, nor was there now time to snatch the great shield from the wall. Still, Conan was better protected than any of his foes except Volmana and Gromel, who were in full armor.

The king glared, puzzled as to their identity. Ascalante he did not know; he could not see through the closed vizors of the armored conspirators, and Rinaldo had pulled his slouch cap down above his eyes. But there was no time for surmise. With a yell that rang to the roof, the killers flooded into the room, Gromel first. He came like a charging bull, head down, sword low for the disembowelling thrust. Conan sprang to meet him, and all his tigerish strength went into the arm that swung the sword. In a whistling arc the great blade flashed through the air and crashed on the Bossonian's helmet. Blade and casque shivered together and Gromel rolled lifeless on the floor. Conan bounded back, still gripping the broken hilt.

"Gromel!" he spat, his eyes blazing in amazement, as the shattered helmet disclosed the shattered head; then the rest of the pack were upon him. A dagger point raked along his ribs between breastplate and backplate, a sword-edge flashed before his eyes. He flung aside the dagger-wielder with his left arm, and smashed his broken hilt like a cestus into the swordsman's temple. The man's brains spattered in his face.

"Watch the door, five of you!" screamed Ascalante, dancing about the edge of the singing steel whirlpool, for he feared that Conan might smash through their midst and escape. The rogues drew back momentarily, as their leader seized several and thrust them toward the single door, and in that brief respite Conan leaped to the wall and tore therefrom an ancient battle-ax which, untouched by time, had hung there for half a century.

With his back to the wall he faced the closing ring for a flashing instant, then leaped into the thick of them. He was no defensive fighter; even in the teeth of overwhelming odds he always carried the war to the enemy. Any other man would have already died there, and Conan himself did not hope to survive, but he did ferociously wish to inflict as much damage as he could before he fell. His barbaric soul was ablaze, and the chants of old heroes were singing in his ears.

As he sprang from the wall his ax dropped an outlaw with a severed shoulder, and the terrible back-hand return crushed the skull of another. Swords whined venomously about him, but death passed him by breathless margins. The Cimmerian moved in, a blur of blinding speed. He was like a tiger among baboons as he leaped, side-stepped and spun, offering an ever-moving target, while his ax wove a shining wheel of death about him.

For a brief space the assassins crowded him fiercely, raining blows blindly and hampered by their own numbers; then they gave back suddenly—two corpses on the floor gave mute evidence of the king's fury, though Conan himself was bleeding from wounds on arm, neck and legs.

"Knaves!" screamed Rinaldo, dashing off his feathered cap, his wild eyes glaring. "Do ye shrink from the combat? Shall the despot live? Out on it!"

He rushed in, hacking madly, but Conan, recognizing him, shattered his sword with a short terrific chop and with a powerful push of his open hand sent him reeling to the floor. The king took Ascalante's point in his left arm, and the outlaw barely saved his life by ducking and springing backward from the swinging ax. Again the wolves swirled in and Conan's ax sang and crushed. A hairy rascal stooped beneath its stroke and dived at the king's legs, but after wrestling for a brief instant at what seemed a solid iron tower, glanced up in time to see the ax falling, but not in time to avoid it. In the interim one of his comrades lifted a broadsword with both hands and hewed through the king's left shoulder-plate, wounding the shoulder beneath. In an instant Conan's cuirass was full of blood.

Volmana, flinging the attackers right and left in his savage impatience, came plowing through and hacked murderously at Conan's unprotected head. The king ducked deeply and the sword shaved off a lock of his black hair as it whistled above him. Conan pivoted on his heel and struck in from the side. The ax crunched through the steel cuirass and Volmana crumpled with his whole left side caved in.

"Volmana!" gasped Conan breathlessly. "I'll know that dwarf in Hell—" He straightened to meet the maddened rush of Rinaldo, who charged in wild and wide open, armed only with a dagger. Conan leaped back, lifting his ax.

"Rinaldo!" his voice was strident with desperate urgency. "Back! I would not slay you—"

"Die, tyrant!" screamed the mad minstrel, hurling himself headlong on the king. Conan delayed the blow he was loth to deliver, until it was too late. Only when he felt the bite of the steel in his unprotected side did he strike, in a frenzy of blind desperation.

Rinaldo dropped with his skull shattered, and Conan reeled back against the wall, blood spurting from between the fingers which gripped his wound.

"In, now, and slay him!" yelled Ascalante.

Conan put his back against the wall and lifted his ax. He stood like an image of the unconquerable primordial—legs braced far apart, head thrust forward, one hand clutching the wall for support, the other gripping the ax on high, with the great corded muscles standing out in iron ridges, and his features frozen in a death snarl of fury—his eyes blazing terribly through the mist of blood which veiled them. The men faltered—wild, criminal and dissolute though they were, yet they came of a breed men called civilized, with a civilized background; here was the barbarian—the natural killer. They shrank back—the dying tiger could still deal death.

Conan sensed their uncertainty and grinned mirthlessly and ferociously. "Who dies first?" he mumbled through smashed and bloody lips.

Ascalante leaped like a wolf, halted almost in midair with incredible quickness and fell prostrate to avoid the death which was hissing toward him. He frantically whirled his feet out of the way and rolled clear as Conan recovered from his missed blow and struck again. This time the ax sank inches deep into the polished floor close to Ascalante's revolving legs.

Another misguided desperado chose this instant to charge, followed half heartedly by his fellows. He intended killing Conan before the Cimmerian could wrench his ax from the floor, but his judgment was faulty. The red ax lurched up and crashed down and a crimson caricature of a man catapulted back against the legs of the attackers.

At that instant a fearful scream burst from the rogues at the door as a black misshapen shadow fell across the wall. All but Ascalante wheeled at that cry, and then, howling like dogs, they burst blindly through the door in a raving, blaspheming mob, and scattered through the corridors in screaming flight.

Ascalante did not look toward the door; he had eyes only for the wounded king. He supposed that the noise of the fray had at last roused the palace, and that the loyal guards were upon him, though even in that moment it seemed strange that his hardened rogues should scream so terribly in their flight. Conan did not look toward the door because he was watching the outlaw with the burning eyes of a dying wolf. In this extremity Ascalante's cynical philosophy did not desert him.

"All seems to be lost, particularly honor," he murmured. "However, the king is dying on his feet—and—" Whatever other cogitation might have passed through his mind is not to be known; for, leaving the sentence uncompleted, he ran lightly at Conan just as the Cimmerian was perforce employing his ax-arm to wipe the blood from his blinded eyes.

But even as he began his charge, there was a strange rushing in the air and a heavy weight struck terrifically between his shoulders. He was dashed headlong and great talons sank agonizingly in his flesh. Writhing desperately beneath his attacker, he twisted his head about and stared into the face of Nightmare and lunacy. Upon him crouched a great black thing which he knew was born in no sane or human world. Its slavering black fangs were near his throat and the glare of its yellow eyes shrivelled his limbs as a killing wind shrivels young corn.

The hideousness of its face transcended mere bestiality. It might have been the face of an ancient, evil mummy, quickened with demoniac life. In those abhorrent features the outlaw's dilated eyes seemed to see, like a shadow in the madness that enveloped him, a faint and terrible resemblance to the slave Thoth-amon. Then Ascalante's cynical and all-sufficient philosophy deserted him, and with a ghastly cry he gave up the ghost before those slavering fangs touched him.

Conan, shaking the blood-drops from his eyes, stared frozen. At first he thought it was a great black hound which stood above Ascalante's distorted body; then as his sight cleared he saw that it was neither a hound nor a baboon.

With a cry that was like an echo of Ascalante's death-shriek, he reeled away from the wall and met the leaping

35

horror with a cast of his ax that had behind it all the desperate power of his electrified nerves. The flying weapon glanced singing from the slanting skull it should have crushed, and the king was hurled half-way across the chamber by the impact of the giant body.

The slavering jaws closed on the arm Conan flung up to guard his throat, but the monster made no effort to secure a death-grip. Over his mangled arm it glared fiendishly into the king's eyes, in which there began to be mirrored a likeness of the horror which stared from the dead eyes of Ascalante. Conan felt his soul shrivel and begin to be drawn out of his body, to drown in the yellow wells of cosmic horror which glimmered spectrally in the formless chaos that was growing about him and engulfing all life and sanity. Those eyes grew and became gigantic, and in them the Cimmerian glimpsed the reality of all the abysmal and blasphemous horrors that lurk in the outer darkness of formless voids and nighted gulfs. He opened his bloody lips to shriek his hate and loathing, but only a dry rattle burst from his throat.

But the horror that paralyzed and destroyed Ascalante roused in the Cimmerian a frenzied fury akin to madness. With a volcanic wrench of his whole body he plunged backward, heedless of the agony of his torn arm, dragging the monster bodily with him. And his outflung hand struck something his dazed fighting-brain recognized as the hilt of his broken sword. Instinctively he gripped it and struck

36

with all the power of nerve and thew, as a man stabs with a dagger. The broken blade sank deep and Conan's arm was released as the abhorrent mouth gaped as in agony. The king was hurled violently aside, and lifting himself on one hand he saw, as one mazed, the terrible convulsions of the monster from which thick blood was gushing through the great wound his broken blade had torn. And as he watched, its struggles ceased and it lay jerking spasmodically, staring upward with its grisly dead eyes. Conan blinked and shook the blood from his own eyes; it seemed to him that the thing was melting and disintegrating into a slimy unstable mass.

Then a medley of voices reached his ears, and the room was thronged with the finally roused people of the court—knights, peers, ladies, men-at-arms, councillors—all babbling and shouting and getting in one another's way. The Black Dragons were on hand, wild with rage, swearing and ruffling, with their hands on their hilts and foreign oaths in their teeth. Of the young officer of the door-guard nothing was seen, nor was he found then or later, though earnestly sought after.

"Gromel! Volmana! Rinaldo!" exclaimed Publius, the high councillor, wringing his fat hands among the corpses. "Black treachery! Some one shall dance for this! Call the guard."

"The guard is here, you old fool!" cavalierly snapped Pallantides, commander of the Black Dragons, forgetting

Publius' rank in the stress of the moment. "Best stop your caterwauling and aid us to bind the king's wounds. He's like to bleed to death."

"Yes, yes!" cried Publius, who was a man of plans rather than action. "We must bind his wounds. Send for every leech of the court! Oh, my lord, what a black shame on the city! Are you entirely slain?"

"Wine!" gasped the king from the couch where they had laid him. They put a goblet to his bloody lips and he drank like a man half dead of thirst.

"Good!" he grunted, falling back. "Slaying is cursed dry work."

They had stanched the flow of blood, and the innate vitality of the barbarian was asserting itself.

"See first to the dagger-wound in my side," he bade the court physicians.

"Rinaldo wrote me a deathly song there, and keen was the stylus."

"We should have hanged him long ago," gibbered Publius. "No good can come of poets—who is this?"

He nervously touched Ascalante's body with his sandalled toe.

"By Mitra!" ejaculated the commander. "It is Ascalante, once count of Thune! What devil's work brought him up from his desert haunts?"

"But why does he stare so?" whispered Publius, drawing away, his own eyes wide and a peculiar prickling among the short hairs at the back of his fat neck. The others fell silent as they gazed at the dead outlaw.

"Had you seen what he and I saw," growled the king, sitting up despite the protests of the leeches, "you had not wondered. Blast your own gaze by looking at—" He stopped short, his mouth gaping, his finger pointing fruitlessly. Where the monster had died, only the bare floor met his eyes.

"Crom!" he swore. "The thing's melted back into the foulness which bore it!" "The king is delirious," whispered a noble. Conan heard and swore with barbaric oaths.

"By Badb, Morrigan, Macha and Nemain!" he concluded wrathfully. "I am sane! It was like a cross between a Stygian mummy and a baboon. It came through the door, and Ascalante's rogues fled before it. It slew Ascalante, who was about to run me through. Then it came upon me and I slew it—how I know not, for my ax glanced from it as from a rack. But I think that the Sage Epemitreus had a hand in it—"

"Hark how he names Epemitreus, dead for fifteen hundred years!" they whispered to each other.

"By Ymir!" thundered the king. "This night I talked with Epemitreus! He called to me in my dreams, and I walked down a black stone corridor carved with old gods, to a stone stair on the steps of which were the outlines of Set, until I came to a crypt, and a tomb with a phœnix carved on it—"

"In Mitra's name, lord king, be silent!" It was the high-priest of Mitra who cried out, and his countenance was ashen.

Conan threw up his head like a lion tossing back its mane, and his voice was thick with the growl of the angry lion.

"Am I a slave, to shut my mouth at your command?"

"Nay, nay, my lord!" The high-priest was trembling, but not through fear of the royal wrath. "I meant no offense." He bent his head close to the king and spoke in a whisper that carried only to Conan's ears.

"My lord, this is a matter beyond human understanding. Only the inner circle of the priestcraft know of the black stone corridor carved in the black heart of Mount Golamira, by unknown hands, or of the phœnix-guarded tomb where Epemitreus was laid to rest fifteen hundred years ago. And since that time no living man has entered it, for his chosen priests, after placing the Sage in the crypt, blocked up the outer entrance of the corridor so that no man could find it, and today not even the high-priests know where it is. Only by word of mouth, handed down by the high-priests to the chosen few, and jealously guarded, does the inner circle of Mitra's acolytes know of the resting-place of Epemitreus in

40

the black heart of Golamira. It is one of the Mysteries, on which Mitra's cult stands."

"I can not say by what magic Epemitreus brought me to him," answered Conan. "But I talked with him, and he made a mark on my sword. Why that mark made it deadly to demons, or what magic lay behind the mark, I know not; but though the blade broke on Gromel's helmet, yet the fragment was long enough to kill the horror."

"Let me see your sword," whispered the high-priest from a throat gone suddenly dry.

Conan held out the broken weapon and the high-priest cried out and fell to his knees.

"Mitra guard us against the powers of darkness!" he gasped. "The king has indeed talked with Epemitreus this night! There on the sword—it is the secret sign none might make but him—the emblem of the immortal phœnix which broods for ever over his tomb! A candle, quick! Look again at the spot where the king said the goblin died!"

It lay in the shade of a broken screen. They threw the screen aside and bathed the floor in a flood of candle-light. And a shuddering silence fell over the people as they looked. Then some fell on their knees calling on Mitra, and some fled screaming from the chamber.

There on the floor where the monster had died, there lay, like a tangible shadow, a broad dark stain that could not be washed out; the thing had left its outline clearly etched in its blood, and that outline was of no being of a sane and normal world. Grim and horrific it brooded there, like the shadow cast by one of the apish gods that squat on the shadowy altars of dim temples in the dark land of Stygia.